MRS. COLE on an ONION ROLL and Other School Poems

by Kalli Dakos
pictures by JoAnn Adinolfi

Simon & Schuster Books for Young Readers

For Alicia, Sarah, Katie, Jarrod, Jackie,
Byron, Jacqueline, Pierce, Nadia and
all the children in our schools
whose love of language
inspired these poems
—K.D.

For Karsten,
my favorite work of art
—J.A.

SIMON & SCHUSTER BOOKS FOR YOUNG READERS
An imprint of Simon & Schuster Children's Publishing Division
1230 Avenue of the Americas
New York, NY 10020
Text copyright © 1995 by Kalli Dakos
Illustrations copyright © 1995 by JoAnn Adinolfi
SIMON & SCHUSTER BOOKS FOR YOUNG READERS
is a trademark of Simon & Schuster.
Designed by Christy Hale
The text of this book is set in Goudy Old Style.
Manufactured in Hong Kong by
South China Printing Company (1988) Ltd.
10 9 8 7 6 5 4 3 2 1
Library of Congress Cataloging-in-Publication Data
Dakos, Kalli.
Mrs. Cole on an onion roll, and other school poems / by
Kalli Dakos ; pictures by JoAnn Adinolfi.—1st ed.
p.   cm.
Summary: A collection of thirty-two poems celebrating life in school.
1. Elementary schools—Juvenile poetry. 2. Children's poetry, American.
[1. Schools—Poetry. 2. American poetry.] I. Adinolfi, JoAnn, ill. II. Title.
PS3554.A414M77   1995
811'.54—dc20   94-8018
ISBN 0-02-725583-2

Contents

Mrs. Cole on an Onion Roll

We're so hungry
That we could eat—

NADIA:
      A chocolate cake
      And a garter snake.

DOUG:
      Carrot sticks
      And toothpicks.

SHELLEY:
      A big pizza pie
      And a tiger's eye.

PIERCE:
      A pound of cheese
      And ninety fleas.

EVERYONE:
      And Mrs. Cole
      On an onion roll!

Mrs. Wren Lost Her Glasses Again

Mrs. Wren
Lost her glasses again,
She's looking everywhere,
Oh! Oh!
I see them in her hair!

Mrs. Wren
Lost her pencils again,
She's looking everywhere,
Oh! Oh!
I see them in her hair!

Mrs. Wren
Lost her students again,
She's looking everywhere,
Oh! Oh!
I see them in her ___!

Tricked ya!
(They're not in her hair,
They're hiding somewhere!)

Frog-a-lert!

Frog-a-lert,
Frog-a-lert,
Six frogs in our class.
Frog-a-lert,
Frog-a-lert,
Brought to school by Cass.

Frog-a-lert,
Frog-a-lert,
Hopping everywhere.
Frog-a-lert,
Frog-a-lert,
See the teacher glare.

Frog-a-lert,
Frog-a-lert,
What a crazy day.
Frog-a-lert,
Frog-a-lert,
Hooray! Hooray!

Love Note

Ashley sends note to Eric:
Smack!
Smack!
I dooooooooooooooooo!
I dooooooooooooooooo!
I send a kiss,
Just for youuuuuuuuuuuuuuuu!

Eric sends note to Ashley:
Yuck!
Yuck!
Poooooooooooooooooo!
Poooooooooooooooooo!
I send the kiss,
Back to youuuuuuuuuuuuuuuu!

The Wiggles Beat the Woggles

The wiggles beat the woggles,
Then the woggles beat the wiggles,
Till we all got the giggles,
Wiggling, woggling round the gym.

Pop! Pop!
The Chicken Pops!

Pop,
Pop,
The chicken pops
Are popping over Drew.

Pop,
Pop,
The chicken pops
Are popping over you!

Pop,
Pop,
The chicken pops
Are popping over Ted!

Pop,
Pop,
The chicken pops
Are sending me to bed!

Peter the Pain

Peter is sitting
Beside me again,
Says I have mush
Instead of a brain,

Steals my pencil
And gives it to Wayne,
Gets me in trouble
With Mrs. McShane.

Move me to China,
To France or to Spain.
Just get me away from

Peter the Pain!

Second-Grade Worms

They wiggle and squiggle all in a pack

from the north to the south then all the way back

they jiggle and twiggle and stir about

I teach second-grade worms there is no doubt!

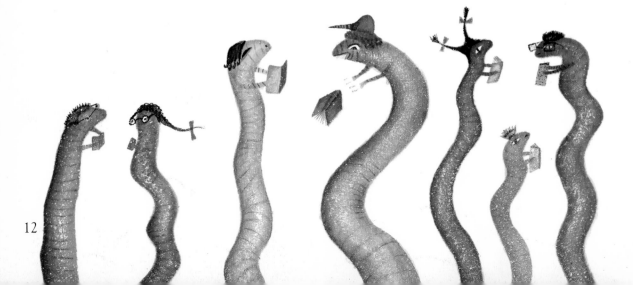

My Teacher

She loves fairy tales,
And poems,
And rocket ships,
And cream cheese,
And cotton candy,
And
ME!

There's a Bug on the Teacher

There's a bug on the teacher,
And it's crawling on her shoe,
What will she do?
It's crawling on her shoe!

There's a bug on the teacher,
And it's crawling on her pants,
Has us in a trance,
That bug on her pants.

There's a bug on the teacher,
And it's crawling on her shirt,
I hope it won't hurt,
That bug on her shirt.

There's a bug on the teacher,
And it's crawling on her neck,
Everyone check,
It's crawling on her neck.

There's a bug on the teacher,
And it's crawling on her nose,
Why do you suppose
It's tickling her nose?

Ah ChOOOOOOOOOOOOOOOOOOOOOOOOOOOOOOOOOOOOOOO!

There's a bug on the floor, and it's heading out the door!

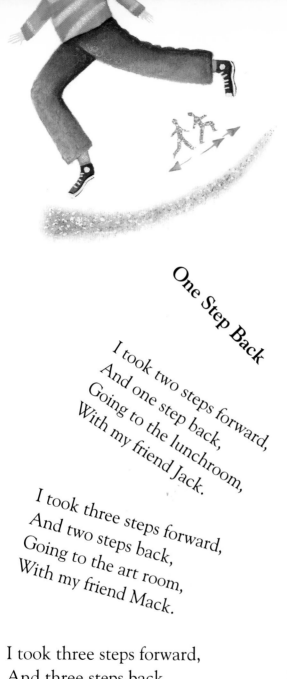

One Step Back

I took two steps forward,
And one step back,
Going to the lunchroom,
With my friend Jack.

I took three steps forward,
And two steps back,
Going to the art room,
With my friend Mack.

I took three steps forward,
And three steps back,
Didn't move at all,
With my best friend, Zack.

Would You Like a Hamburger or a Cheeseburger?

TEACHER:
> Fred, Would you like
> A hamburger
> Or a cheeseburger?

FRED:
> I'd like a cheeseburger,
> Without the cheese,
> Please.

Loooooooooong Names

In our classroom
We like loooooooooooooong names
And short names.
Our hamster is called
Rolypoly Ravioli, the Third,
And our goldfish is called
G.

Five Seconds Left in the Game

We were playing basketball.
The Frogs were tied
With the Toads,
And there were only
Five screaming seconds
Left in the game
When a Toad
Grabbed the ball.

$$0.05 = bounce$$
$$0.04 = bounce$$
$$0.03 = bounce$$
$$0.02 = bounce$$
$$0.01 = basket$$

$$0.00$$

| Toads 7 |
| Frogs 5 |

The Frogs cried:
Oh! Noooooooooooooooooo!

The Toads cheered:
One, two, three, four,
We just got
The winning score!
Five, six, seven, eight,
We're the best,
We're really great!

Give us a T   T
Give us an O   O
Give us an A   A
Give us a D   D
Give us an S   S

What does it spell?
Toads!
Louder!
Toads!
Yeah! Yeah!

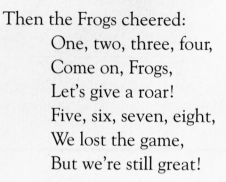

Then the Frogs cheered:
       One, two, three, four,
       Come on, Frogs,
       Let's give a roar!
       Five, six, seven, eight,
       We lost the game,
       But we're still great!

Give us an F   F
Give us an R   R
Give us an O   O
Give us a G   G
Give us an S   S

What does it spell?
Frogs!
Louder!
Frogs!
Yeah! Yeah!

20

In Trouble

In art,
Sarah painted
Her fingers yellow,
And she did not get in trouble.

Jonathan
Poured green water
All over his desk,
And he did not get in trouble.

Katie painted
An apple
From her lunch box black,
And she did not get in trouble.

I was being perfectly good,
And I got in trouble!

Oh, all right,
So I did paint Kathy's nose green.
It looks nice, doesn't it?

My Favorite Pencil

JENNIFER:
> My
> favorite
> pencil
> is
> long
> and
> thin
> and
> has
> an
> eraser
> where
> it
> begins.

SYLVIA:
> My favorite pencil
> Is short and fat
> And has an eraser
> For a hat.

22

SANTOS:

My favorite pencil broke in two, and I tried to fix it up with glue.

An Itty-bitty Speck of a Dot

All that's left of the
Eraser I bought
Is an itty-bitty
Speck of a dot.

●

Turn On the Darkness

Turn on the darkness,
Take away the light,
My head is getting heavy,
My eyes are closing tight.

Turn on the darkness,
Take away the light,
I'm sleepy in class,
And I want to say
Good-night,
    Good-night,
        Good-night,
            Good-night.
                Good . . .

Oh,
Ms. Jones,
The answer to the question?
What question?

The Day Before I Wear the Birthday Crown All Day in School

Sometimes,
Even a day
Seems too far away.

25

Hip Hip Hooray!

Sally brought a flower
For the teacher today,
And the teacher yelled,
"Hip hip hooray!"

Byron brought an apple
For the teacher today,
And the teacher yelled,
"Hip hip hooray!"

Jennifer brought a poem
For the teacher today,
And the teacher yelled,
"Hip hip hooray!"

Jarrod brought a candy
For the teacher today,
And the teacher yelled,
"Hip hip hooray!"

Ben brought a radish
For the teacher today,
And the teacher said,
"A radish?
Why a radish?"

And Ben said,
"Because I love radishes!"

Ben brought a radish
For the teacher today,
And the teacher yelled,
"Hip hip hooray!"

Muddy Recess

I love the mud!
I do!
I do!
I love to squish
It on my shoe!

To slip!
To slide!
Through puddles fast,
If only
All this mud
Could last!

The Bumbling Day

I'm bumbling my way,
Through a bumbling day.

Bumble 1:
Crashed into Ms. Lunn.

Bumble 2:
Papers stuck with glue.

Bumble 3:
Spilled my teacher's tea.

Bumble 4:
Lost the tug-of-war.

Oh, no!
CRASH!
BANG!
Ouch!

Bumble 5:
Am I still alive?

Tall Saul

When you call me

Tall
Saul

I could call you

**Pee Wee
Lee,**

But I don't.

Elemenopee

Elemenopee,
Elemenopee,
What in the world
Is an elemenopee?

Hint: A B C D E F G H I J K _ _ _ _ _ _

Knit 1, Purl 2

Knit
1
purl
2

We
love
to
knit,
we
really
do.

Knit
2
purl
1

Making
a
scarf
is
lots
of
fun.

Knit
4
purl
3

It's
too
long
for
you
or
me.

Knit
2
purl
4

Now
it's
big
enough
for
a
dinosaur.

Knit
6
purl
10

How
do
we
stop
and
start
again?

This Day Is Going to Be Very Loooooooooooooooong

I did math all morning,
But my work's all wrong.
This day is going to be
Very loooooooooooooooooooooooooong!

Four against One

Is four
Against one
Fair,
Anywhere?

YAHOOOOOOOOOOOOOOOOOOOOOOOOOOOOOOOOO!

When my teacher said,
"You passed your test,"
I jumped on my desk,

And yelled,

"YAHOOOOOOOOOOOOOOOOOOOOOOOOOOOOOOO!"

Surprised myself,
And my teacher,
TOOOOOOOOOOOOOOOOOOOOOOOOO!

I Lost My Tooth in My Doughnut

I lost my tooth in my doughnut,
When it wiggled and I screamed, "Ow!"
I lost my tooth in my doughnut,
I must have eaten it somehow.
I lost my tooth in my doughnut,
Will the tooth fairy still come now?

Dear Tooth Fairy,
I ate my tooth.
It was a mistake.
Please still come,
Or my heart will break.
Yours truly,
Bob

Dear Bob,
Thanks for the note,
And the tooth you drew.
I've left a treat,
And it's just for you!
Yours truly,
The Tooth Fairy

37

My Project's in the Toilet

My project's in the toilet,
I dropped it by mistake,
Now I am
           plunge,
                   plunge,
                           plunging,
Till my hands and arms ache.

It was a little carving,
Of an evergreen tree,
That got stuck in the toilet,
By mistake, by me.

My project's in the toilet,
I hope it doesn't break,
Now I am
           plunge,
                   plunge,
                           plunging,
Till my hands and arms ache.

There's Something in My Book Bag, and It's Slimy

There's something in my book bag,
And it's slimy.
There's something in the dark,
Deep
Down
There.

There's something
In my book bag,
And it's slimy.
Teacher,
Will you check?
Do
You
Dare?

You're an Author Now

I'm writing,
I'm writing,
I'm writing in my book.
I'm writing,
I'm writing,
Oh, Teacher, come and look.

You're writing,
You're writing,
Your story sure looks great.
You're writing,
You're writing,
To read it, I can't wait.

I'm writing,
I'm writing,
It's magic somehow.
I'm writing,
I'm writing,
I'm an author now.

You're writing,
You're writing,
I'm glad you've learned how.
You're writing,
You're writing,
You're an author now!